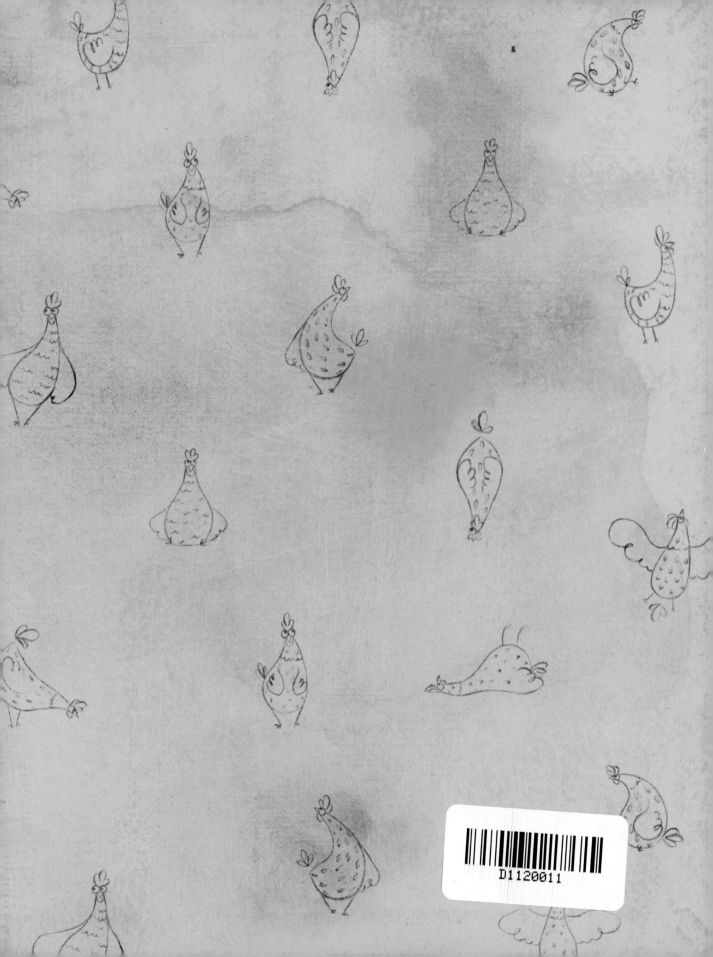

GWEN

THE RESCUE HEN

Written by **Leslie Crawford**

Illustrated by **Sonja Stangl**

Hen's eyes pop open. She has been dreaming again. For just that
moment, the in-between time when you're leaving a dream and not
quite awake, Hen is happy.

In her dream, she can spread her wings wide, as wide as they can go.
Then she flaps them, the way she's always wanted to, and lifts herself
off the ground.

In her dream, she can fly.

But Hen is awake now. She looks in front of her, to the left, to the right, up and down. Everywhere, so many chickens! Just like her, sitting here, day after day, with barely enough room to turn around.

She doesn't remember how she got here. She doesn't remember being born, but who does? All she knows is that she's always been in this place,

Suddenly, a chilly draft slides over Hen, giving her goosebumps. Which is funny since she's a chicken. But this is no laughing matter.

Because Hen hears something, something big.

HOWOOOOH!

The wind is howling, so loudly the chickens start to squawk and screech, warning each other to *run!*

But of course they can't run. All they can do is stay, trembling to the very ends of their feathers.

The noise grows into a monstrous roar.

The big chicken house starts to shake.

Pop! Pop! Pop! The doors burst open.

Whoosh! The roof flies away.

KABOOM!

In an instant, Hen's cage is aloft. Hen has never been on an amusement ride, of course, but this is what it feels like, terrifying and thrilling, twirling and whirling through space, thinking you might be doomed.

I might be doomed! thinks Hen.

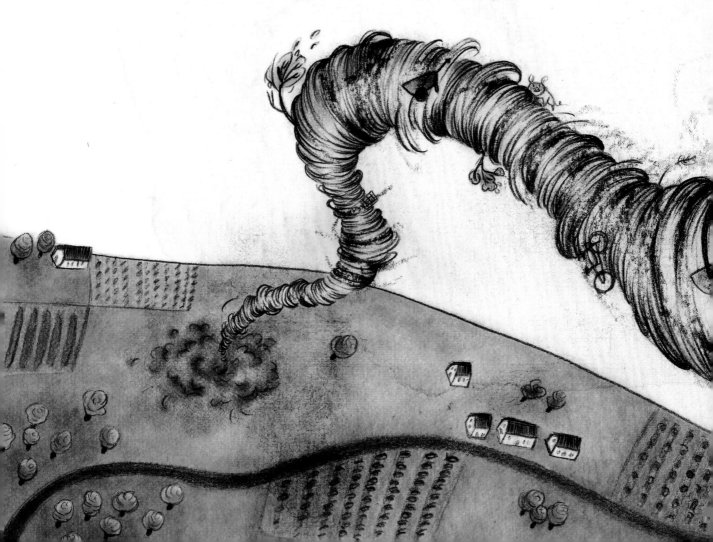

CLONK!

The cage has landed. Hen struggles to get rightside up.

What is this place? She blinks, taking it all in.

Sunlight. It streams into the cage. Colors, so many colors. The greenest greens, yellowest yellows, and reddest reds.

Swooosh! Hen watches a silvery rush of flapping wings soar just beyond her cage, before disappearing into the sky...

BRAAAK! says Hen. The biggest chicken she has ever seen is staring at her.

Bak, Hen says to her. Bak, bak, say the other chickens.

The big chicken doesn't say peep.

Hen cocks her head, confused. Chickens always talk to each other. Something is very wrong with this one. (Besides her being so enormous!)

Bak? She tries one last time. Nothing.

Just then, another strong gust blows.

The cage teeters...

topples...

... then plunges to the ground.

Oooof! That hurt! Hen's feathers are ruffled, but she's in one piece.

Cluck, cluck, cluck, cluck, cluck? Hen asks.
Cluck, cluck, cluck, cluck cluck. *Check.* Everyone is okay.

Then she sees it. The open door!

Hen takes a step. Then another.

For the first time ever, Hen is outside her cage in the fresh, breezy air.
She basks in the warmth of the sun. She shakes her feathers, catching
the wind in them.

She sees a patch of bright green grass and bends to take a bite when...

RRUFF, RRUFF!

SQUAWK!

The chickens scatter in every direction, and Hen discovers how quickly she can run. But whatever is coming after her is fast, too.

Hen feels his hot breath on her tail.
She flaps her wings in a wild panic.

"Bix! Come!"

"Did you see what I saw?" the girl says. "Was that a chicken?"

"Yeah, that was crazy," the boy says. "I thought chickens were, you know, *chicken*."

"Maybe Bix is the chicken," the girl laughs. "Come on, buddy, we gotta go. See you later!"

"Hey there, chicken. Come on out. I won't hurt you, promise."

Hen freezes.

"Chicken, it's not safe for you to be out here all alone."

Hen doesn't budge.

"Are you hungry? I don't know if this is what chickens like, but it's all I have."

I'm hungry. But maybe he is, too. And he might eat me.

Hen stays put.

"Sorry, chicken, but I can't wait anymore. I have to go."

Finally! I thought he'd never leave.

But no sooner does Hen step out from her safe place when...

VAROOOM!

Has any chicken ever had a day like this?!

Hen begins flapping her wings, and before she even knows what she's doing, she's in the air.

I did that! Hen thinks. *I flew.*

"Chicken! Hey, chicken! That was close!"

"My name is Mateo," says the boy. "How about I call you Gwen? That's my house. It's a lot nicer than a tree branch. Want to come over?"

Gwen, of course, has no idea what Mateo is saying.

She looks at the boy. She sees his bike and admires its sparkly feathery streamers. And because chickens can detect even the tiniest of things from far away, she notices that Mateo has scattered more cookie crumbs.

But that's not the only reason she decides to hop down from the tree and follow Mateo home. Deep inside Gwen, something is happening. She's starting to trust this boy.

It takes time to make a real friend, especially if one of the friends is a chicken and the other is a person.

Mateo figures out what chickens do. And Gwen figures out what chickens do, too.

She likes to take dust baths.

And lift herself in the air.

And preen.

And roost.

Mateo also learns that chickens love being with other chickens. "Gwen, look who I found!" Gwen can hardly believe her eyes. It's her old friends.

Mateo names them Jen, Sven, Renn, Zen, and Adrienne. Gwen cackles and lets him know how happy it makes her to be part of a flock.

She lets Mateo know he's part of her flock, too.

And on days like this one, after a busy afternoon spent scratching for bugs to eat, kicking up enough dust for a bath, and counting all her chickens, she hops on another bike ride with Mateo.

"Come on, Gwen," says Mateo, as he helps settle her onto the handlebars. *Let's hit it!* she thinks. *Let's fly.*

And off they go.

More about chickens

Chickens are good at math. From a young age, they can add, subtract, and recognize different shapes.

A chicken's superpower is her eyesight. It's much better than our own. They can see four wavelengths: blue, green, red, and UV light. Humans can see only red, blue and green. They're also better at sensing motion, which makes it easier to spot, and pounce, on tiny bugs. Each eye moves independently, which lets chickens see what's going on around them without turning their heads.

They've got a good sense of time. Chickens know when it's dinnertime and can become annoyed if the people who feed them are even a few minutes late.

Chickens are flock animals who like company. A group of three or four is enough to let them develop a comfortable pecking order. The perks to being head chicken include getting the best place to roost and the choicest bits of food.

Chickens are pretty smart. They can be taught many tricks, including how to ride on bikes, come when called, and play the piano. They have good memories and can remember the people and birds they like even after many months spent apart. They can also recognize up to 100 other chickens.

Chickens can feel each other's happiness or fear. If one of them observes another sad chicken, she's likely to feel sad, too.

Each chicken has a personality. Some are nervous and shy, others as friendly as dogs. But generally speaking, chickens are curious and resourceful, especially when it comes to finding food.

Chickens have their own language. They use up to 24 different sounds to communicate. Tuck-tuck-tuck means *I've found food!* Bak-bak-bak means *It's time for dinner.* A brak, or squawk, can signal danger. If you pet a chicken, she may purr like a cat. After laying an egg, a chicken will sing her egg song to proudly announce her achievement.

Brown or white eggs? You can often tell what color egg a chicken lays by the color of her earlobes. (Yes, chickens have earlobes!) So birds with white earlobes typically lay white eggs. Those with brown earlobes lay brown eggs.

Chickens like dust baths. (Not water baths.) It's part of how birds preen, or groom themselves, to keep their feathers in good condition. The dust absorbs excess oil and prevents feathers from matting.

Birds are descended from dinosaurs, specifically, a group of two-legged dinosaurs known as therapods. This means a chicken is distantly related to the towering Tyrannosaurus Rex!

Chickens can fly, kind of. Even the best flyers rise only high enough to clear a fence or reach a low branch. Fortunately, **they can run!** As fast as nine miles an hour.

Gwen the Rescue Hen is a fantastical tale inspired by the hens who managed to survive after a series of tornadoes demolished a huge egg-laying farm in Croton, Ohio.

Thanks to the following good people for reviewing *More about chickens:*
Sy Montgomery, author, *Birdology*
Lauri Torgerson-White, senior animal welfare specialist, Mercy for Animals

STONE PIER
PRESS

Stone Pier Press
San Francisco, California

ISBN - 9780998862323
Library of Congress Control Number: 2018944367
Names: Crawford, Leslie, author. Stangl, Sonja, illustrator. Ellis, Clare, editor.
Title: Gwen the Rescue Hen
Summary: Gwen discovers the joys of being a hen after she's sprung from an egg-laying farm by a fierce tornado, and finds her way to a boy named Mateo - for ages 4 to 7.

Manufactured in China by Shenzhen Reliance Printing.

10 9 8 7 6 5 4 3 2 1
First Printing: July 2018
Printed on Forest Stewardship Council (FSC) responsibly sourced paper from well-managed forests